FOR JOE
—J.S.

FOR CURTIS AND BEN,
SASHA AND JESSAMIN,
NAT AND DEBORAH,
AND CATMANDU (the best fly-catcher in the business)
—E.K.

THIS IS A BORZOI BOOK PUBLISHED BY ALFRED A. KNOPF

Copyright © 2006 by Judy Sierra
Illustrations copyright © 2006 by Edward Koren

Published in the United States by Alfred A. Knopf, an imprint of Random House Children's Books,
a division of Random House, Inc., New York.

Library of Congress Cataloging-in-Publication Data
Sierra, Judy.
Thelonius Monster's sky-high fly pie / Judy Sierra ; illustrations by Edward Koren. — 1st ed.
p. cm.
SUMMARY: A good-natured monster thinks a pie made out of flies would be a good
dessert and invites all his friends and relatives over to try it.
ISBN: 0-375-83218-1 (trade) — ISBN: 0-375-93218-6 (lib. bdg.)
ISBN-13: 978-0-375-83218-5 (trade) — ISBN-13: 978-0-375-93218-2 (lib. bdg.)
(1. Monsters—Fiction. 2. Pies—Fiction. 3. Stories in rhyme.)
I. Koren, Edward, ill. II. Title.
PZ8.3.S577Th 2006
(E)—dc22
2005016773

MANUFACTURED IN CHINA

10 9 8 7 6 5 4 3 2 1

First Edition

THELONIUS MONSTER'S MONSTER'S SKY-HIGH FLY PIE

A revolting rhyme

by **Judy Sierra**

with delicious drawings

by **Edward Koren**

Alfred A. Knopf
New York

THELONIUS MONSTER

once swallowed a fly,

and decided that flies would taste

grand in a pie.

That silly guy!

THELONIUS urgently

e-mailed a spider.

He wanted advice from a savvy insider.

"You'll need something sticky" was her reply.

"To catch a fly."

THELONIUS MONSTER concocted a goo

of molasses and sugar and honey and glue,

and he rolled out a crust of astonishing size.

Now for the flies...

WANTED
FLIES
ONLY

THELONIUS stealthily followed

a

horse

and a

dog

and a
cat

and a
COW...

. . . and, of course, he dived in a Dumpster,

he circled a sewer,

and spent several hours near a pile of manure.

He lured h u n d r e d s
and t h o u s a n d s
of succulent flies,

and their footsies all stuck

to his fly-catching pie.

Perhaps they'll die.

THELONIUS MONSTER addressed invitations to all his disgusting-est friends and relations.

PLEASE COME TO MY MANSION
THIS SUNDAY FOR PIE.

DON'T WEAR A TIE.

On Sunday, THELONIUS opened the door
to *eleventeen*

ravenous
m o n s t e r s,
or more—

his aunties,

his uncles,

his cousins,

his chums.

"How it **glistens!**"

they shouted. "And listen—

it **hums!**

It's the tunefullest pie

that has ever been made.

We shall march to the

buzz in a

monster

parade."

As they picked up their forks

and they circled the room,

the pie full of flies lifted off with a

VOOM.

Up, up the staircase

it *whirred* and it *whined*

with all of the monsters galumphing behind.

It *whizzed* out the window.

It *whooshed* to the sky.

Bye-bye, fly pie!

THELONIUS MONSTER started to cry,

"Now no one will taste my

sensational pie."

(For though it had taken him so long to make it,

the monster had somehow forgotten to **bake** it.)

But then, by a stroke
of incredible luck,

in the sky all the flies'

little feet came unstuck.

When the pie *fell* to earth in a huge cloud

of dust,

e l e v e n t e e n

monsters

devoured the crust.

His creepiest cousin declared with a roar,

"A DESSERT LIKE THIS

NEVER EXISTED BEFORE—

A PIE THAT COULD SPARKLE,

COULD SING, AND COULD SOAR.

IT'S DESPICABLY SWEET

(WITH A SLIGHT HINT OF FLY).

YOU'RE A FABULOUS COOK!

YOU'RE A WONDERFUL GUY!"

"We love your pie!"

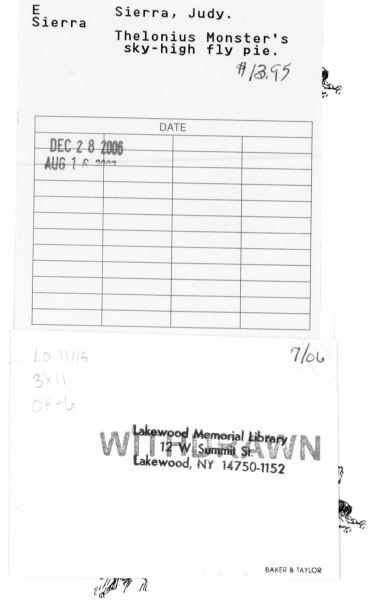

Sierra, Judy.

Thelonius Monster's
sky-high fly pie.

$13.95

DATE			
DEC 2 8 2006			
AUG 1 6 2007			

LO 11/15
3×11
OP+6

7/06

BAKER & TAYLOR